Family Story Collection

⎯⎯⎯⎯⎯⎯∞∞∞⎯⎯⎯⎯⎯⎯

Confidence Is Key

STORIES ABOUT HELPING OTHERS AND BEING YOURSELF

⎯⎯⎯⎯⎯⎯∞∞∞⎯⎯⎯⎯⎯⎯

Book Four

Printed in China
First Edition
1 3 5 7 9 10 8 6 4 2

ISBN 0-7868-3528-1

For more Disney Press fun, visit www.disneybooks.com

Book Four

---❄❄❄---

Confidence Is Key

---❄❄❄---

STORIES ABOUT HELPING OTHERS AND BEING YOURSELF

Introduction

Self-confidence is the key to a good self-image. Children build confidence through trial and error. Inevitably, they will make mistakes. But with gentle guidance from the adults around them, children can learn from their mistakes and develop faith in their ability to succeed.

In "King-in-Training," Simba's curiosity gets the better of him when he pushes boundaries and ventures farther from his home than he should. This puts him and his friends into a dangerous situation. Melody, in "Who's the Real Thief?" wants to remain a mermaid at any cost and imperils her loved ones in the process. Both lion cub and child take responsibility for their actions, and work to correct the problems they create, a vital step toward becoming confident adults.

King-in-Training

from *The Lion King*

———∽∼∼∞∽∼———

Be confident, but don't take unnecessary risks.

Mufasa had warned his son Simba not to venture outside the Pride Lands. But then Simba's dastardly uncle, Scar, tempted the young lion by telling him about the Elephant Graveyard that lay beyond a rise at the northern border. Adventurous Simba just had to see it! Together with his friend, Nala, Simba went to explore the area.

"It's creepy," said Nala as they walked up to a huge elephant skull.

"Yeah," Simba replied. "Isn't it great?"

Just then, Zazu the bird caught up with
them. It was his job to look after Simba and
Nala, and they had been trying to lose him
all morning.

"We're beyond the boundary of the Pride
Lands," he told Simba. "We are in danger."

Simba just smiled. "I laugh in the face of
danger. Ha!"

Then, from the shadows, they heard voices. Simba, Nala, and Zazu watched nervously as three hyenas approached.

"Well, well, well," said Shenzi the hyena. "What have we got here?"

"The future king!" Simba declared proudly.

The hyenas were unimpressed. "Do you know what we do to kings who step out of their kingdom?" Shenzi said threateningly.

At first, Simba did not think the hyenas could harm him. After all, he was Mufasa's son! But then Zazu explained that they were on the hyenas' land—and at their mercy.

Simba, Nala, and Zazu made a break for it, darting away from the hyenas and through the Elephant Graveyard.

"Did we lose 'em?" Nala asked Simba, panting.

"I think so," Simba replied.

But Zazu was missing! The hyenas had caught him. Simba and Nala went back for him. They lured the hyenas away from Zazu, but then the hyenas started to chase them.

Before long, the hyenas had the young lions cornered. Nala hid behind Simba as the hyenas closed in.

Suddenly, Mufasa leaped out of the shadows. His mighty roar echoed through the graveyard as he fought the hyenas. They were no match for the Lion King, and the hyenas pleaded for mercy. Mufasa warned them to stay away from his son before letting them go.

Simba could not look his father in the eye after what had happened.

"Simba, I'm very disappointed in you," Mufasa said when they had gotten back home. "You disobeyed me. And what's worse, you put Nala in danger."

Simba felt terrible, and he began to cry. "I was just trying to be brave like you," he said.

Mufasa looked

down at his son. "I'm only brave when I have to be," he explained. "Simba, being brave doesn't mean you go looking for trouble."

Simba still had a few things to learn about being a king. But with his father's loving guidance, he would someday have the strength and maturity to follow in his footsteps.

Who's the Real Thief?

from *The Little Mermaid II: Return to the Sea*

Trust your first impressions.

A riel's daughter, Melody, was thrilled when Morgana magically turned her into a mermaid. But there was just one problem.

"There wasn't enough potion for this to be a *forever* potion," Morgana said sadly. "I could make the spell last longer if I had my magic trident. But it was stolen years ago, and there's no one to get it back for me." Then Morgana told Melody that King Triton, the ruler of the sea, had the trident.

Melody hated the thought of returning to her ordinary life. "Maybe I could get it back for you," she suggested.

"You would do that for me?" Morgana asked.

"I'll bring back your trident," Melody promised.

And with the help of her friends, Tip the penguin and Dash the walrus, Melody found her way to Atlantica.

The three sneaked into King Triton's castle

and hid beneath a table just as the king entered the room. "That must be him," Melody whispered to her friends. "But he doesn't look like a thief."

Despite the fact that Morgana had told her that King Triton had stolen the trident, Melody couldn't shake the feeling that he was a good person. He looked so kind.

Suddenly, Melody spotted the trident. "Look, there it is!"

When King Triton left the room, Melody swam over to the trident. It was beautiful. And for some reason, it looked familiar to Melody.

"The king's coming back!" cried Dash.

Melody shook off the feeling and grabbed the trident. Then she and her friends swam to safety.

Morgana was waiting back in her cave. "Clever girl! You've brought my trident!" she exclaimed.

After Melody handed over the trident, Morgana began laughing maniacally.

"The power of the seven seas is now at my command!" she cried. "You've been a naughty girl—stealing from your own grandfather!"

Melody gasped. "My grandfather?"

The kind-looking merman hadn't stolen the trident from Morgana after all. Instead, Morgana had tricked Melody into stealing it from him. She should have never trusted Morgana or gone against her own instincts.

As Morgana turned Melody back into a human, Ariel and King Triton arrived, along with their friends. But the trident gave Morgana the power to command all the creatures of the sea. They could do nothing to stop her.

Just as all seemed lost, Melody realized something—with her legs back, she was no longer "of the sea." She could defeat Morgana! And this time, she wasn't going to ignore her instincts. She sneaked up and snatched the trident from Morgana, then returned it to King Triton.

Melody felt bad about helping Morgana, but her family was quick to forgive her. She hugged her grandfather for the first time.

Now, Melody would no longer have to

choose between the land and the sea. With
Morgana defeated and her family together
again, she could have the best of both
worlds!